CITY CAT, COUNTRY CAT

◆ Patricia Cleveland-Peck ◆
Illustrated by Gilly Marklew

Morrow Junior Books
NEW YORK

First published in the United States 1992 by Morrow Junior Books.
Published by arrangement with HarperCollins Publishers.
The author and/or illustrator asserts the moral right
to be identified as the author and/or illustrator of this work.

Printed in Great Britain by B.P.C.C. Paulton Books
1 2 3 4 5 6 7 8 9 10

Library of Congress Cataloging-in-Publication Data
Cleveland-Peck, Patricia.
City cat, country cat / Patricia Cleveland-Peck ; illustrated
by Gilly Marklew.
p.   cm.
Originally published in England under the title: Freckle and Clyde.
Summary: A country boy and a city girl discover they've been sharing
a cat for a long time without knowing it.
ISBN 0-688-11644-2 (trade)—ISBN 0-688-11645-0 (library)
1. Cats—Juvenile fiction.   [1. Cats—Fiction.]   I. Marklew, Gilly,
ill.   II. Title.
PZ10.3.C59914Ci   1992
[E]—dc20   91-42402   CIP   AC

Freckle lived in the country at Willow Farm. He slept in the sun, caught mice, and (when he felt like it) played with David Percy.

Charlie lived in the city at 12 East Avenue.

He slept by the fire,

and (when he felt like it) played with Sarah Smith.

In the mornings Freckle enjoyed creamy milk from the dairy.

As soon as David's dad started up the milking machines, he would appear.

At night Charlie enjoyed canned cat food from
the supermarket. As soon as Sarah's mom opened
the can, he would be there. But one evening, Charlie
wasn't around at dinnertime.

"Never mind," said Sarah's mom. "You know he
sometimes goes away for days. He'll be back. Cats
lead their own lives. You don't have to worry."

Sure enough, the next day, there was Charlie stretched out on the rug when Sarah came home from school.

One day David went looking for Freckle.
"I wish I could get him to sleep on my bed," said David.
"Not him!" said David's dad. "He's an outside cat,
a stray. I expect he's out in the fields chasing rabbits.

"Don't worry, he'll be back. Cats have their own lives to lead, you know."

And sure enough, the next morning, there was Freckle, waiting for his milk as usual.

Sometimes Charlie curled up on the sofa with Sarah,
or suddenly jumped on her in bed and purred,

so that the house seemed full of cats. Other times
he was missing when she wanted to cuddle him.

Sometimes it looked as if Freckle pounced
and played in the hedges, rushed up trees,

and hid in the wildflowers all at the same time,
so that the farmyard seemed full of cats.

Other times David looked for Freckle in vain.
"He's snug in a barn somewhere," said David's dad.

"Cats see to themselves. Don't fuss, he'll be back."
And he always was.

Then Charlie took to being away for longer and longer periods.

"He's off in the woods somewhere," said Sarah's mom. "Don't worry. Cats look after themselves. He'll be back."

And he always was.

"If you could talk, would you tell me where you go?" asked Sarah. But Charlie just flicked the end of his tail without waking up.

Then Sarah had an idea. She would follow him and see where he went. She would track him and learn what he was up to.

She watched and watched, but Charlie just stayed in the garden. He snoozed in the shrubbery or curled up in the catnip or dozed among the delphiniums.

Then, very early one morning, Charlie suddenly
sprang down off the windowsill and jumped
over the garden wall. He trotted up the path,
past the school, through the woods, across
the bridge over the stream, around a big field,
through a hole in the hedge, across a little field,
under a gate, and into the yard of Willow Farm.

All the while Sarah followed, trying hard
not to be seen. She was getting very mad.
And when she saw Charlie saunter right into
the barn, she finally lost her temper.
She marched across the yard, calling out
in a loud voice,

"You've got my cat!"

David came out of the barn.

"No, there's only our cat here," he replied, amazed.

"A white cat with a splotch of black over one eye?" asked Sarah.

"Yes, that's my Freckle," said David.
"No, it's my Charlie," insisted Sarah.

"Come in and see," said David's mom, trying to smooth things over. "He was a stray, it's true, but he's been here for ages...."

Freckle (or Charlie) was lapping his milk. He gazed from Sarah to David and from David to Sarah. Then very slowly he began to wash his face.

In the end they agreed to share him, to let him come and go as he pleased (which, of course, he fully intended to do anyway). For, as everyone knows, cats lead their own lives, sometimes even double lives.